All Ladybird books are available at most bookshops,
supermarkets and newsagents, or can be ordered direct from:

Ladybird Postal Sales
PO Box 133 Paignton TQ3 2YP England
Telephone: (+44) 01803 554761
Fax: (+44) 01803 663394

A catalogue record for this book is available
from the British Library

Published by Ladybird Books Ltd
A subsidiary of the Penguin Group
A Pearson Company

© 1998 Cosgrove Hall Films

Based on The Animal Shelf created by Ivy Wallace

LADYBIRD and the device of a Ladybird are trademarks of
Ladybird Books Ltd Loughborough Leicestershire UK

The Animal Shelf™

Gumpa Solves a Jigsaw Puzzle

BASED ON THE ANIMAL SHELF CREATED BY
IVY WALLACE

Ladybird

One fine day Timothy's Special Animals were using his magnifying glass.

"Look, Little Mut's turned into Big Mut!" laughed Woeful. They were playing at being detectives.

"Do you want to help me to solve a jigsaw puzzle?" asked Timothy.

The Animals said they would and followed him out into the sunshine.

Soon they were all crowding round the jigsaw puzzle, and it kept them busy all afternoon.

"Look at that!" exclaimed Woeful, laying down one of his pieces. "Brilliant!" And he was so excited that he hurled his hat up into the air.

Just then Timothy was called in to tea. "Come on, we've got to clear up," he said, and started to pick up the pieces.

"But I've got another piece ready!" wailed Woeful. "It's not fair!" Then he kicked out crossly at the box of jigsaw pieces.

"Woeful, sometimes you go too far," said Timothy, telling him off. "Come on, we need all those pieces back in the box."

"Sorry," said Woeful. Then he picked up his hat and helped the others to tidy up.

That evening there was plenty of time to try the jigsaw again.

At last they needed just two more pieces.

"I've got one," said Gumpa. "How about that?"

"Very good," answered Timothy. "Now who's got the last piece?"

But none of them had, and it was too late to find it now.

"Goodnight," said Timothy to his Animals, and they all went unhappily to sleep.

Next morning there was still a hole in the jigsaw. But Detective Gumpa had thought of a plan to solve the mystery of the missing piece!

First he led the Animals back to the scene of the crime. Then they asked one another questions. Next they followed some trails, and when they had finished finding their own footprints, they split up to look for other clues and suspects.

Woeful interviewed Jick the Jackdaw, but he only took shiny things from the garden.

Stripey and Getup questioned Squirrel, but he just showed them an acorn!

Little Mut and Gumpa followed a trail to Mrs Mole's cave. Detective Gumpa was certain the little moles would have hidden the jigsaw piece.

The Animals met together again in the garden. "The only place we haven't looked is under Mrs Mole's new molehill," announced Gumpa.

Woeful flattened the ground at once. "Nothing," he said, disappointed, and took off his hat in disgust.

Everyone looked at Woeful.

"The missing jigsaw piece!" exclaimed Stripey, pointing to Woeful's head where his hat had been.

"Yes, that's definitely it!" said Gumpa, examining the jigsaw piece with the magnifying glass.

Later the Animals told Timothy what had happened.

"I hope you've learnt your lesson, Woeful. Being bad tempered only causes trouble," said Timothy.

"Sorry," said Woeful.

"I liked being a detective, though," said Gumpa grandly. "I solved the mystery of the missing jigsaw piece!"

Gumpa helped Woeful to place the last piece and then everyone cheered. The jigsaw was complete at last.